D0567620

THE
STAR WARS®
TRILOGY SCRAPBOOK
THE GALACTIC EMPIRE

by Mark Cotta Vaz

SCHOLASTIC INC.

New York   Toronto   London   Auckland   Sydney

To Allan Kausch, Keeper of the lore of the Star Wars universe
(and immune to the lure of the dark side).

ACKNOWLEDGEMENTS

The Force is also with Lucasfilm publishing guru Lucy Autrey Wilson
and stellar editor Jane Mason. My appreciation to Cara Evangelista
and Tina Mills for helpful connections and guidance while at
Skywalker Ranch. Much forceful thanks as well to the Scholastic
editorial team of Jennifer Johnson and Susan Kitzen.

No part of this publication may be reproduced in whole or in part, or stored in a retrieval system, or transmitted in any form or by any
means, electronic, mechanical, photocopying, recording, or otherwise, without written permission of the publisher.
For information regarding permission, write to Scholastic Inc., 555 Broadway, New York, NY 10012.

ISBN 0-590-12052-2

TM & ® & © 1997 Lucasfilm Ltd.
All rights reserved. Published by Scholastic Inc.

Book design by Todd Lefelt

12 11 10 9 8 7 6 5 4 3 2 1   7 8 9/9 0 1 2/0

Printed in the U.S.A.
First Scholastic printing, November 1997

INTRODUCTION:
THE DARK SIDE

The Imperial City of Coruscant! Its sky-scrapers and pyramids stretch to the horizon from the base of the Manarai Mountains, a mighty snow-covered range covering much of the planet. For as long as records exist, this planet has been the capital of the galaxy, this city the seat of the government known as the Old Republic. The hundreds of generations of Republic leaders formed a link to the founding dreams of peace and justice for all. And always ready to defend the Republic from the forces of evil were the noble Jedi Knights. It was a Golden Age, and many believed it would last forever.

But eventually this legacy was swept away. A dark shadow of evil fell across the galaxy. The democratic government of the Old Republic was dissolved. The Jedi Knights were hunted down and destroyed. And glittering, glorious Coruscant became the citadel of an evil Galactic Empire.

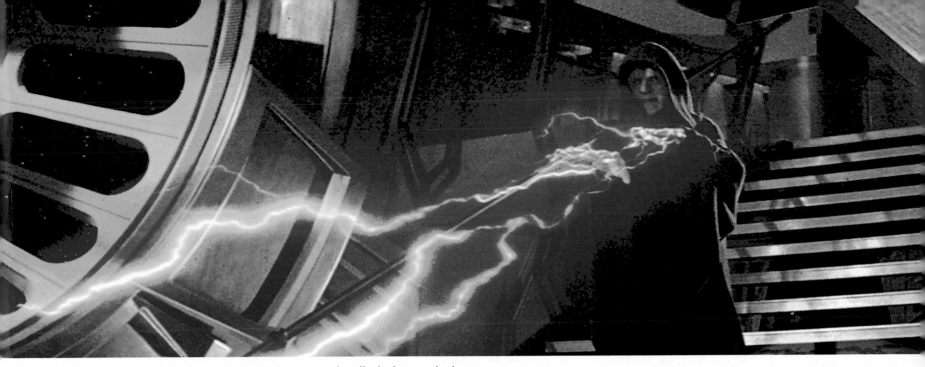

Emperor Palpatine, whose very gesture can emit deadly lightning bolts!

Darth Vader, flanked by two Imperial Royal Guards.

The twilight of the Old Republic began with the bloody Clone Wars, in which the Jedi Knights battled and defeated the mysterious Mandalore warriors. Two of the Republic's great heroes from the conflict were General and Jedi Knight Obi-Wan Kenobi and Anakin Skywalker, Obi-Wan's prize student. Although the Republic had triumphed in the wars, the glory of victory was brief. The institutions of the Republic itself were rotten with corruption. The old ways of peace and justice were quickly being forgotten.

A young senator named Palpatine was called upon to save the Republic. Palpatine was made President of the Republic and began to restore order to the galactic government. But as Palpatine's power grew, so did his ambition. His greed for power became an obsession. Before he could be stopped, Palpatine had crowned himself Emperor and the Republic had been replaced by Palpatine's "New Order." At the Emperor's right hand would be Anakin Skywalker, seduced to evil and transformed into Darth Vader.

The long age of peace and justice was over. The dark times had begun.

COMMAND FORCE
A N D
CITADELS OF EVIL

I

When the Republic was swept away, the traditions of peace and justice were replaced with the Empire's rule by fear and military strength. The Emperor surrounded himself with ruthless men who would carry out his brutal wishes. Military posts were established on many planets throughout the galaxy. The Empire's war ships constantly patrolled the territories. And Palpatine ordered the construction of deadly war machines.

But the Empire's dark conquest did not go unchallenged. The Alliance to Restore the Republic (the Rebel Alliance) strongly opposed the Empire. This group of freedom fighters was formed by some of the last incorruptible leaders of the Old Republic. Together they began to build a movement, enlisting the help of individuals, worlds, and even star systems in the fight against Imperial power. Furious that anyone would defy his rule, the Emperor ordered that the Rebels be crushed.

Thus began the great Galactic Civil War. At stake was the fate of the entire galaxy.

Vader's Star Destroyer chases after a ship bearing Rebel leader Princess Leia Organa.

The gigantic Destroyer swallows up Leia's ship.

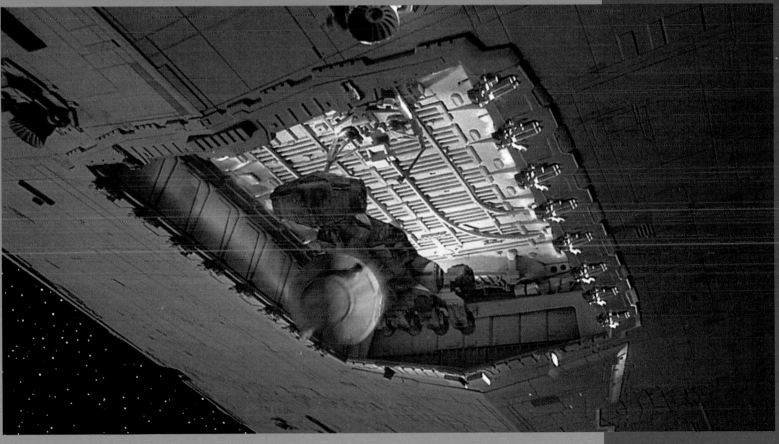

IMPERIAL LEADERS

EMPEROR PALPATINE

One of the great mysteries of the Imperial era was how a simple politician such as Palpatine transformed himself into the ruthless Emperor. Few knew that Palpatine had discovered the dark side of the Force.

The Force is an energy field generated by all living things. It surrounds and penetrates everything, binding the galaxy together. The Jedi Knights embraced the light side of the Force and the spiritual serenity found there. But the Force had a dark side as well. The dark side is the way of anger, fear, and aggression.

With the dark side to guide him, Palpatine was a ruthless leader. His rule would see the development of the most horrible war weapon ever created: the Death Star, a gigantic battle station powerful enough to destroy an entire planet.

Although he ruled the galaxy from Imperial City, Emperor Palpatine also had special throne rooms at every Imperial stronghold and aboard every Star Destroyer starship.

IMPERIAL ROYAL GUARD

The Emperor is protected at all times by the Royal Guards, who wear flowing red robes, full body armor, and red helmets. Little is known about these mysterious attendants, but each of them is chosen for his size, strength, intelligence, and loyalty to the Empire. Once selected to serve as Royal Guards, these soldiers receive additional training in weapons and hand-to-hand combat. It is even whispered that the highest-ranking guards (called Imperial Sovereign Protectors), who serve as the Emperor's personal bodyguards, have been trained in the dark side of the Force. But all who wear the red helmet and robe of the Imperial Royal Guard are sworn to fight unto death to protect their master, the Emperor.

Imperial Royal Guards positioning themselves outside an Imperial shuttle as Vader waits for the Emperor to emerge.

DARTH VADER
DARK LORD OF THE SITH

When Obi-Wan Kenobi tried to teach young Anakin Skywalker the ways of the Force, his student became frustrated. His progress was so slow! Mastering the light side of the Force required time and patience. The dark side, however, presented a quicker way to the awesome power of the Force.

Obi-Wan made one last try to save Anakin from the dark side, but Anakin drew his Jedi weapon—the lightsaber, with its blade of pure energy. Obi-Wan reluctantly raised his own lightsaber in defense, and the two battled near a pit of molten lava. During the fight, Skywalker fell into the molten pit. But Anakin Skywalker did not die. He emerged from the pit a scorched shell of a man, full of hatred. In that dark moment, Anakin was transformed.

Vader in the meditation chamber he uses for both relaxation and life support.

The molten fires had singed Anakin's lungs, requiring him to wear a special black helmeted mask and life-supporting body armor. Over the armor he wore a sweeping black cloak. Anakin had become Darth Vader, master of the dark side and Dark Lord of the Sith.

Although Vader, at Palpatine's command, hunted down and killed nearly all the Jedi Knights, a few escaped. Obi-Wan fled to the arid wastelands of the desert planet Tatooine. Yoda, a Jedi Master and Obi-Wan's own teacher, escaped to the swamp world of Dagobah.

When the Rebellion posed a threat to the Emperor's rule, Palpatine ordered Vader to hunt down and destroy the Alliance leaders.

GRAND MOFF WILLHUFF TARKIN

During the last days of the Old Republic, Tarkin was governor of the Seswenna Sector. By the time Palpatine ascended to the Imperial throne, Tarkin was one of his key advisors. Tarkin's personal belief in rule by fear convinced the Emperor to disband the Old Republic's Senate. Tarkin oversaw the design and construction of the first Death Star, and was named its commander when the battle station became operational. At the height of his power, Tarkin even gave orders to the mighty Lord Vader. When Rebels destroyed the first Death Star, Tarkin was killed.

COMMANDERS

The Emperor trusted ruthless subordinates like Vader and Tarkin to enforce his will. But throughout the military system there were other commanders in charge of Star Destroyers, garrisons, and various Imperial projects. These men were commanders in name only, and were easily replaced. The Emperor ruled by fear, and the price of failure was death.

Vader uses the Force to relieve these low-level officers of their commands — and their lives!

STRONGHOLDS

The Imperial presence was everywhere in the galaxy. Gigantic Imperial Star Destroyers patrolled every territory. Military garrisons transformed whole worlds into armed camps. It was almost as if the entire galaxy was in the palm of the Emperor's hand. Squeeze that hand into a fist and the Rebels would be crushed!

Stormtrooper patrols were in the forefront of direct military action. Here a patrol searches a stretch of desert on the planet Tatooine for a Rebel starship escape pod that might contain stolen plans for the Death Star.

A trooper scans the sands atop a dewback, a reptilian creature native to Tatooine.

Floating in the cloudy atmosphere above the planet Bespin is the mining and trading outpost of Cloud City. Known for its ethereal beauty and entertainment complexes, Cloud City was also an officially neutral colony in the Galactic Civil War. But neutrality didn't stop Vader and his stormtroopers from taking control of the city when it suited Imperial purposes.

A garrison of stormtroopers watches over Lobot, the cyborg aide to Cloud City administrator Lando Calrissian.

Towering in height, ruthless and physically threatening, Darth Vader was a symbol of the Emperor's New Order, a figure of supreme power and evil. Vader's helmeted breathing mask and black armor made him seem more machine than man.

As a Master of the dark side of the Force, Vader was expert at wielding a lightsaber. With a forceful gesture, Vader could send a wave of energy powerful enough to stop an enemy from breathing or send objects flying through the air. But deadliest of all was Vader's ruthless will. Nothing could stop him from carrying out the commands of his master the Emperor.

Not only did Vader commune with the dark side, he was also known as Dark Lord of the Sith. The Sith were ancient masters of occult forces. Back in the glory days of the Old Republic, the cult of the Sith had been established by Jedi Knights who had turned to the dark side.

Before he became Darth Vader, Anakin Skywalker fathered twins, a son and a daughter. Kept from him, they would grow into two of the greatest leaders of the Rebellion: Luke Skywalker and Princess Leia Organa. One of Vader's orders from the Emperor would be to capture Luke and turn him to the dark side. If Luke wouldn't turn to the dark side, Vader was prepared to kill him.

FIREPOWER:
LAND AND SPACE

II

The Old Republic had the guardian strength of Jedi Knights. The Empire enforced its ruthless decrees with Imperial soldiers, stormtroopers, and a massive arsenal that included Star Destroyers and the terrifying Death Star. The Emperor could command these forces from throne rooms scattered throughout the galaxy.

A single Imperial command could send starships to the far side of the galaxy, usher in an invasion of stormtroopers, even order the superlaser of the Death Star to destroy an entire planet.

A Star Destroyer and TIE fighters, with the Death Star under construction.

STORMTROOPERS

The shock troopers of the Empire, stormtroopers look like robots in their white helmeted masks and armored spacesuits. Each trooper is prepared to die for the Imperial cause.

Stormtrooper units can adapt themselves to the special demands of each planet they patrol.

Specially trained snowtroopers led by Darth Vader take command of a Rebel base on the ice planet Hoth.

Wild creatures on different planets are often tamed and used as beasts of burden by stormtroopers. This dewback is on patrol in the Tatooine dunes.

On the forest moon of Endor, a stormtrooper zips through the thick forests on a low-flying speeder bike.

19

Several classes of probe droids, also called pro-bots, assist in Imperial surveillance. Probots are equipped with sensors, various measuring devices, and antigravity propulsion units that allow them to fly.

This giant probot moves across the frozen landscape of Hoth. It would uncover the Rebel presence on Hoth, report back to the command ship, and then self-destruct just as Rebel hero Han Solo fired a shot.

When the Imperial forces attack on land, they often use the gigantic All Terrain Armored Transport, or AT-AT. Sometimes called a "walker," this powerful machine is impervious to blaster fire and can march through most defensive lines. On rough terrain, the Empire also uses the All Terrain Scout Transport, or AT-ST. Sometimes called a "chicken" or "scout walker," the AT-ST moves on two mechanical legs and can travel quickly through rugged areas.

ALL TERRAIN ARMORED TRANSPORT (AT-AT)

The AT-AT stands almost fifteen meters tall and is outfitted with protective metal plating. It moves like a four-legged mechanical monster. Its head area includes the crew deck and gunner's station, and is equipped with blaster cannons.

This giant walker is seen at an Imperial station on the forest moon of Endor.

ALL TERRAIN SCOUT TRANSPORT (AT-ST)

The scout walkers are seven meters tall and can move quickly on their two mechanical legs. These chicken walkers are also equipped with their own blaster cannons.

An AT-ST on the forest moon of Endor. The chicken walkers move nimbly through thick forests and other rugged landscapes.

The Empire rules the galaxy with a formidable array of starships. Imperial firepower ranges from mighty Star Destroyers to single-pilot TIE fighters.

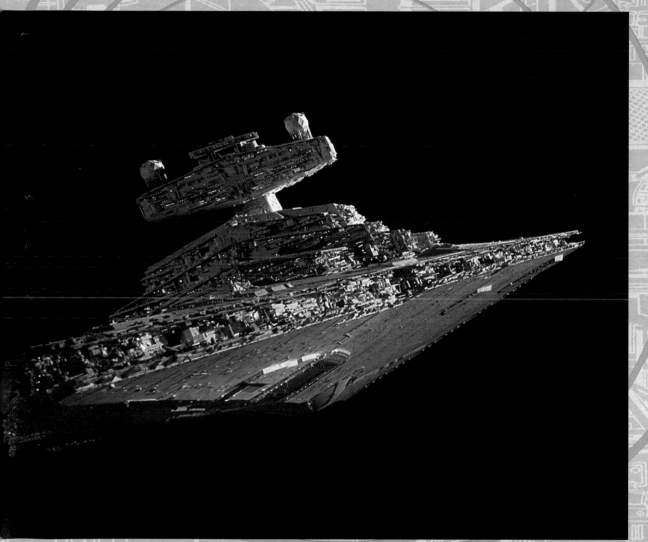

STAR DESTROYERS

These triangular-shaped starships are equipped with turbolasers and ion cannons. They are so big they can hold detachments of Imperial soldiers and stormtroopers, TIE fighters, landing barges, shuttles, ground assault vehicles, specialized droids, and other equipment.

There are two classes of Star Destroyer: *Imperial* class and *Super* class.

The Imperial Star Destroyer is more than one-and-a-half kilometers long. The ship pictured here—the *Devastator*—was commanded by Darth Vader. In the early stages of the Civil War, the *Devastator* captured Princess Leia's consular ship over Tatooine in hopes of reclaiming the Death Star plans stolen by the Rebel forces. (Leia had placed the stolen Death Star technical readouts in the memory banks of the droid R2-D2. Accompanied by the droid C-3PO, R2 entered an escape pod and landed on Tatooine.)

The Super Star Destroyer is more than eight kilometers long! It features enough firepower to reduce a planet's surface to rubble. The mightiest Star Destroyer of all is Darth Vader's personal *Super*-class ship, the *Executor*. This ship is five times larger than the *Imperial*-class ships, and was the first of this new class of ship. Only the Death Star battle station is bigger than this awesome battleship.

TIE FIGHTERS

The Empire's main combat starfighter. Although TIEs cannot travel great distances, they are easily deployed against specific targets from land bases, Star Destroyers, or the Death Star. Each TIE features twin six-sided solar-panel wings. These panels provide energy for the ship, and power two laser cannons. The central command pod seats a single pilot. In contrast to the mighty Star Destroyers and the Death Stars, TIE fighters are quick and maneuverable.

A fleet of TIE fighters leaves the second Death Star.

TIE INTERCEPTOR

With its bent-wing design, this new class of starfighter looks slightly different from the basic model. The interceptor is built with more speed and power, and includes four laser cannons instead of two. This first model was personally designed for Darth Vader, who used it in aerial combat against Rebel starfighters during the Battle of Yavin.

TIE interceptor in battle in the trench of the first Death Star.

THE DEATH STAR

The supreme weapon in the universe. During the course of the Galactic Civil War, the Empire would build two Death Stars. The first fully operational of these battle stations would deliver a crushing blow to the Rebel Alliance by obliterating the peaceful planet Alderaan. The second Death Star would be barely operational during the Battle of Endor.

THE FIRST DEATH STAR

This battle station was designed as a symbol of Imperial power. The armor-shelled, sphere-shaped structure was the size of a small moon. Inside it could house a million soldiers, more than 7,000 TIE fighters, and a vast array of other weapons. But its main weapon was a superlaser . . . powerful enough to blow an entire planet to bits.

Here we see the Death Star in the distance. Note its size in relation to the giant planet Yavin.

Here Han Solo's ship, the *Millennium Falcon*, is being pulled toward the Death Star by a magnetic tractor beam.

Grand Moff Tarkin,
Death Star commander.

THE SECOND DEATH STAR

Despite its awesome power, the first Death Star would be destroyed by two blasts from a Rebel X-wing starfighter piloted by Luke Skywalker. The Death Star plans stolen by the Alliance revealed a fatal weakness: a surface exhaust port that connected to the power core. A direct hit into this opening from a pair of proton torpedoes fired by Luke set off the chain reaction that destroyed the Death Star.

The second Death Star was designed without the vulnerability that destroyed the first battle station. It would be bigger in every way, with a more powerful superlaser. As the Galactic Civil War raged on, Emperor Palpatine himself would visit the Death Star during its construction. From a special throne room in the new battle station, Palpatine would direct his final plan to defeat the Rebellion.

The second Death Star under construction above the Sanctuary Moon of Endor.

The Emperor rules from the throne room of the second Death Star.

Death Star docking bay (with an Imperial shuttle).

With great power comes great responsibility. So it was in the days of the Old Republic, when everyone had a stake and a share in peace and justice. The Emperor's New Order changed that. Instead of freedom for the star systems, the Imperial government enforced its own absolute rule. Anyone who disagreed with his tyranny was forced to accept it.

The Republic and the Jedi Knight tradition practiced compassion, love, and trust. But the Empire's rule meant ruthless use of military power. Vader had begun this pattern of destruction by slaying the Jedi Knights. As we will see, even an entire planet would be destroyed as the Empire tightened its grip on the galaxy.

Below, Vader reviews stormtroopers in anticipation of Emperor Palpatine's arrival. Much of the Emperor's power came from the many millions who followed him without questions. These faceless stormtroopers — and the masked Vader himself — had no identity outside of their allegiance to the Emperor.

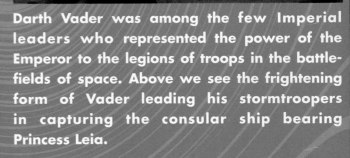

Darth Vader was among the few Imperial leaders who represented the power of the Emperor to the legions of troops in the battle-fields of space. Above we see the frightening form of Vader leading his stormtroopers in capturing the consular ship bearing Princess Leia.

The Dark Lord confronts Princess Leia.

III

DARK ALLIES:
THE UNDERWORLD

One of the secrets of the Imperial era was the dark connection between the Empire and the galactic underworld. Assassins, smugglers, robbers, and bounty hunters were often used by the Empire to further its evil aims.

UNDERWORLD HAUNTS

Underworld beings live in the shadows. But they are not invisible. There are places scattered throughout the galaxy where those with money can go to hire a smuggler or an assassin. The isolated Outer Rim Territory planet Tatooine has long been a favorite underworld haunt. Although still in the shadow of the Empire, the desert world is of little strategic importance to the Imperials. The criminal element on Tatooine can be found in a rough-and-tough bar in the spaceport town of Mos Eisley, as well as in the palace of the crime lord Jabba the Hutt.

MOS EISLEY CANTINA

Jedi Knight Obi-Wan Kenobi called Mos Eisley a "wretched hive of scum and villainy." Most of these villains tend to gather in the smoky confines of the cantina bar. R2-D2 and C-3PO wait outside the cantina, since the place doesn't serve droids.

Snapshots of some of the cantina's underworld regulars:

Dice Igebon (a Florn Lamproid) and Ketwol
(a Pacithhip) chat in the cantina.

Duros, a species accustomed to
space travel. Known to haul cargo
and supplies on behalf of the Empire.

This devilish-looking bounty hunter
is Djas Puhr, a Sakiyan.

JABBA'S PALACE

Out in the Tatooine desert, at the edge of the Dune Sea, sits the palace of Jabba the Hutt.

R2-D2 and C-3PO approach Jabba's palace.

Deep within the dimly lit halls of Jabba's palace, we see Rebel hero Han Solo — imprisoned in a slab of carbonite!

A successful Jabba relaxes on his palace throne.

BIB FORTUNA
Jabba's chief lieutenant, Fortuna, is always at his master's side.

Gamorreans are known for their husky size and bad temper. A number of them serve Jabba as guards. Here we see a grim Gamorrean standing watch on Jabba's sail barge.

SALACIOUS CRUMB
This shameless creature is Jabba's court jester. His cackling laugh and practical jokes always amuse the evil crime lord.

The Max Rebo Band entertains Jabba's court.

Lead singer Sy Snootles and the palace dancers put on a show.

A yuzzum performer. This species inhabits the forest floor of Endor's Sanctuary Moon.

This musician from the planet Rodia helps make the band swing during the palace revelry.

Even when Jabba's throne room rocks with laughter and music, danger is never far away. Anyone who displeases Jabba can find themselves suddenly dropped into the pit below. There dwells the monstrous rancor, the only known creature of its kind. The rancor is one of Jabba's prized possessions.

BOUNTY HUNTERS

Bounty hunters track down and kill or capture their victims for a price. To succeed in this deadly business, a bounty hunter must be smart, a superb pilot, and handy with a blaster. Bounty hunters not only work for crime lords such as Jabba, but also serve the needs of the Empire.

Here is a glimpse of the Empire's underworld connection. Darth Vader, frustrated in his attempts to capture Luke Skywalker, has called for the galaxy's best bounty hunters to track down Luke's friends. With Han, Leia, Chewie, and the droids as bait, Vader hopes to set a trap for the young Rebel hero. Assembled with Vader on the bridge of the *Executor* are (from left to right): Dengar, IG-88, Boba Fett, and Bossk.

Boba Fett and assassin droid IG-88. This infamous class of droids was designed with advanced combat abilities and a warlike temper. The first models reportedly killed their own creators!

Vader and Dengar. Dengar is a personal enemy of Luke's friend Han Solo.

Greedo, a Rodian bounty hunter, confronted Han Solo in the Mos Eisley Cantina. Jabba felt Han had crossed him, and had put a bounty out on the smuggler's head. Greedo planned to collect it.

In an exchange of blaster fire, Solo's shot took out Greedo. (Sudden death is an on-the-job hazard for all bounty hunters.)

Boba Fett, the masked bounty hunter whose exploits are known throughout the galaxy. He is a feared martial arts expert and a crafty tracker. Of all the bounty hunters hired by Vader, it was Fett who successfully tracked Luke's friends to Cloud City.

Fett fires his wrist laser. Fett's battle suit also includes a jet pack, a rope that can be fired to snare an opponent, and rocket darts. His outfit is a rare piece of battle armor once worn by the Mandalore warriors who battled the Jedi Knights during the Clone Wars. How Fett came to possess this battle-scarred super suit remains a mystery.

BOUSHH THE BOUNTY HUNTER

One of many bounty hunters to pass through Jabba's palace. This particular bounty hunter is significant in the annals of the Galactic Civil War for one reason: This is not Boushh, but Princess Leia disguised as the bounty hunter!

Leia's bounty hunter disguise was part of an attempt to rescue Han Solo when he was imprisoned in Jabba's palace.

Pictured here (left-to-right) aboard the Death Star are: Vader, Leia, Grand Moff Tarkin, and Admiral Motti, senior Imperial commander in charge of operations on the Death Star.

After Darth Vader captured Princess Leia's consular ship, he brought Leia to the first Death Star and imprisoned her. Vader and Tarkin would then attempt to force Leia to reveal the location of the secret Rebel base.

At Tarkin's touch, the Princess tries to turn away in disgust.

Vader confronts Leia in the detention block prison chamber. The floating black orb in the background is an Imperial interrogator droid. This cruel weapon was part of the plan to get Leia to reveal Rebel secrets. But the Princess was strong and managed to resist the interrogation. Leia would later be rescued by Luke Skywalker and Han Solo during a daring raid on the Death Star.

After Boba Fett tracked Han's *Millennium Falcon* to Cloud City, Darth Vader could spring his trap to capture Luke Skywalker. The plan almost worked, but Luke was rescued and escaped Cloud City. Han Solo was not so lucky. Here we see him being tortured on Cloud City.

In this Cloud City carbon-freezing chamber, gases from the planet Bespin could be frozen in carbonite for transportation. For the first time a human would be frozen in carbonite — Han Solo!

Lando Calrissian, administrator of Cloud City and an old friend of Han, checks Han's carbonite form. Han is frozen into the carbonite block, but is still alive.

Boba Fett leads the carbonite Han to his ship, the *Slave I*, for the journey to Jabba's palace on Tatooine. (Later, Leia helps rescue Han by disguising herself as a bounty hunter.)

IV

DARK TRIUMPHS

The outcome of the Galactic Civil War turned on a few major battles. Both the Empire and the Alliance had their share of successes. Throughout the conflict, Emperor Palpatine was supremely confident that the Empire would triumph. Palpatine was convinced the Rebel Alliance would be crushed and Luke Skywalker would be turned to the dark side.

DESTRUCTION OF PLANET ALDERAAN

While Princess Leia was a prisoner on the first Death Star, she witnessed one of the Empire's most horrible crimes. Leia had been captured while on a mission to contact Obi-Wan Kenobi on Tatooine and bring the Clone War general to Alderaan, Leia's adopted home world and haven for the Alliance. Now Grand Moff Tarkin threatened to test the Death Star's superlaser . . . by destroying Alderaan!

Here Leia gazes at a monitor showing Alderaan as the superlaser begins to warm up.

The Death Star in range of Alderaan, a jewel of a world shimmering in space. After the horrors of the Clone Wars, Alderaan had renounced military weaponry and embraced a path of peace. Alderaan was one of the few planets that had completely dismantled its war-making powers and banished all weapons. Although Alderaan hadn't officially joined the Alliance, it was supportive of the Rebellion.

The Death Star superlaser gears up . . .

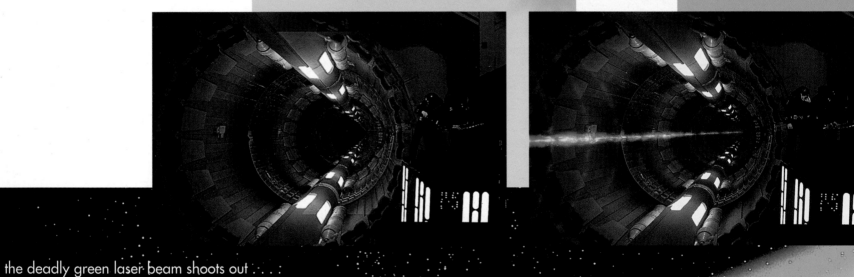

the deadly green laser beam shoots out . . . .

the superlaser beam strikes the planet. In an instant, Alderaan is blown to smithereens.

En route to Alderaan in Han Solo's *Millennium Falcon*, Obi-Wan was staggered as he felt the destruction of the planet. "I felt a great disturbance in the Force, as if millions of voices suddenly cried out in terror and were suddenly silenced," Obi-Wan told his friends. After blasting through hyperspace to the Alderaan system, the *Falcon* crew saw that the entire planet had been reduced to chunks of floating rock.

BATTLE OF HOTH

One of the most stunning defeats suffered by the Rebellion. The Alliance had been on the run from the Imperial forces for years, and hoped that this inhospitable world of freezing wind, snow, and ice would be the perfect hiding place.

Luke Skywalker out in the freezing climate of Hoth, riding a native tauntaun.

Rebel fighters on the ice planet Hoth.

The Imperial invasion of Hoth begins! Here Rebel troops hunker down in an ice trench as the Imperial forces approach.

Echo Base troops under Imperial fire.

As blaster cannon fire from the Imperial walkers pounds them, Rebel fighters take aim at the advancing Imperial forces.

Leading the Imperial ground assault are the gigantic mechanical AT-AT's. As they advance, they mercilessly fire their blaster cannons.

Fighting back, the Rebels attack with armored flying snowspeeders.

The Rebels are forced to retreat.

The Rebels begin the evacuation from Echo Base.

Darth Vader claims Echo Base and victory on behalf of the Empire.

No planet or star system was safe from Imperial might. In the case of Cloud City of Bespin, an Imperial invasion led by Darth Vader forced administrator Lando Calrissian to betray his old friend Han Solo. In exchange for Lando's support, Vader promised that the Empire would leave the Bespin system in peace.

The *Millennium Falcon* enters Cloud City air space and flies down to a landing platform, unaware that an Imperial trap awaits.

Lando soon realizes that Vader was double-crossing him. The Empire would not leave the Bespin system in peace, but would turn Cloud City into an armed Imperial camp. With Han Solo already in the clutches of bounty hunter Boba Fett, Lando and the remaining heroes—Luke, Leia, Chewbacca, and the droids—barely managed to fight their way out and escape Cloud City.

Solo, Leia, and friends are escorted to a dining room. They enter and find themselves face-to-face with Darth Vader! Here Han Solo fires a blaster shot, but the Dark Lord easily deflects it.

Here we see a stormtrooper standing tall beside a fallen comrade, returning Rebel blaster fire.

One of the great side stories of the Galactic Civil War was Darth Vader's battle with his son, Luke Skywalker. Vader planned to turn Luke to the dark side. But the Dark Lord of the Sith also had the opportunity for a rematch with Obi-Wan, his old master and foe.

VADER VS. OBI-WAN

Here we see Obi-Wan walking a corridor of the first Death Star. Obi-Wan sensed that Darth Vader himself was nearby, waiting for their final battle.

The last time Vader and Obi-Wan had crossed their lightsaber blades, Vader was still young Anakin Skywalker and Obi-Wan was his master. "Now I am the master," Vader announced to Obi-Wan as their sabers clashed. "Only a master of evil, Darth," Obi-Wan replied.

During their fight, Obi-Wan had proclaimed, "You can't win, Darth. If you strike me down, I shall become more powerful than you can possibly imagine." When Obi-Wan saw that Luke and his friends were boarding the *Falcon* to escape the Death Star, he silently dropped his lightsaber. Vader's deadly lightsaber blade sliced through the Jedi Knight. But Obi-Wan's strange comment would prove prophetic. He was truly one with the Force and would help Luke Skywalker grow as a Jedi Knight.

VADER VS. LUKE SKYWALKER

Luke would continue his Jedi training on the lonely planet Dagobah. His teacher would be Jedi Master Yoda, who had long ago trained Obi-Wan. It was in a dark cave on Dagobah that Luke had a supernatural encounter with Darth Vader. Luke's lightsaber struck down Vader, but Vader was only an apparition. Luke saw the Vader helmet break open. It revealed Luke's own face! The dreamlike incident was a warning to Luke. Part of him was attracted to the dark side. He was still too young and inexperienced to hope to confront and defeat the dark power of mighty Vader.

But when Luke learned that his friends were in trouble on Cloud City, he instantly decided to rush to their rescue. Yoda and the ghost of Obi-Wan tried to convince Luke not to leave. It was admirable that Luke wanted to help his friends, but he would be rushing into certain doom, the two teachers warned. And while he might save his friends, the future of the Rebellion could be destroyed. But Luke wouldn't listen. He and R2-D2 flew off in the X-wing, bound for Cloud City . . . and Darth Vader's trap.

Despite his youth, Luke put up a valiant effort against the Dark Lord.

Vader uses the Force to send objects flying at Luke, who crashes through a window and finds himself hanging on in the reactor shaft.

Vader reveals that he is Luke's father! Luke is horrified as Vader urges his son to join him. The Dark Lord even proclaims that together they can rule the universe as father and son.

Luke loses his grip and falls down the reactor shaft. Desperate, he clings to a weathervane at the bottom of Cloud City. From there he sends a mental message to Princess Leia. Lando and Leia are escaping from Cloud City in the *Falcon*, but manage to make a miraculous rescue of the defeated Luke.

EPILOGUE:
SHADOWS OF THE EMPIRE

There is an old saying: "The bigger they are, the harder they fall." And so it was with the Empire. Despite its great armies and weapons, the resourceful Rebels managed to find a weakness in the Imperial armor during several decisive battles.

In the Battle of Yavin, Rebel starfighters attacked the open trench of the first Death Star. Pilot Luke Skywalker (with spiritual guidance from Obi-Wan) fired the torpedoes that caused the chain reaction that destroyed the huge battle station. Grand Moff Tarkin, who had refused to evacuate during the Rebel attack, died instantly in the explosion.

In the Battle of Endor, the Alliance not only destroyed the second Death Star, but finally broke the Empire's grip on the galaxy. Han Solo led a group that disabled a shield generator protecting the Death Star, while Lando Calrissian flew the *Millennium Falcon* on a daring attack that blew up the Death Star's fusion core reactor.

And it was in the second Death Star's throne room that Luke Skywalker had his final confrontation with Darth Vader and the Emperor. Luke won without resorting to anger or aggression, even when the Emperor tried to destroy him. Desperate and in agony, Luke appealed to the part of Vader that was still the loving Anakin Skywalker. Vader heard his son, and at the last moment saved Luke by throwing the Emperor into a giant elevator shaft.

Imperial City, Coruscant. Celebration! In this famed city, and throughout the galaxy, crowds of revelers celebrate the defeat of the Empire.

But it would be dangerous to underestimate the power of the dark side. The galaxy is a vast place, with many shadowy areas. There are always those who care nothing for peace and justice, but thirst for the chance to dominate others.

Thankfully there is a bit of Jedi wisdom to balance the threat of evil. As Obi-Wan says, "The Force will be with you—always!"

Author's Credits

Mark Cotta Vaz has written two other books in this Star Wars Trilogy Scrapbook series: *The Complete Star Wars Trilogy Scrapbook* and *The Rebel Alliance Scrapbook*. His other Lucasfilm books include *Secrets of Star Wars: Shadows of the Empire* and *From Star Wars to Indiana Jones: The Best of the Lucasfilm Archives* (with Shinji Hata).